The Children of the Chapel and the First Christmas

Written by
E. G. Enga

Illustrated by
Lora Schaunaman

En Route Books and Media, LLC
Saint Louis, MO

⊕*ENROUTE*
Make the time

En Route Books and Media, LLC

5705 Rhodes Avenue

St. Louis, MO 63109

Cover and interior illustrations credit:

Lora Schaunaman

ISBN-13: 979-8-88870-192-8

Library of Congress Control Number: 2024940294

Dedication

For my mom and my grandma—
I love you both so much! You inspire me every day
and I couldn't have done it without you!

Table of Contents

Chapter 1.. 1

Chapter 2.. 5

Chapter 3.. 8

Chapter 4.. 12

Chapter 5.. 17

Chapter 6.. 31

Chapter 7.. 36

Chapter 8.. 41

Chapter 9.. 49

Chapter 10.. 54

Chapter 11.. 65

Chapter 12.. 78

Chapter 13.. 88

Chapter 14.. 96

Points of Reference 102

Acknowledgments 104

About the Author.. 107

Chapter 1

"Brrr," shivered eight-year-old Zelie Langford. She and her siblings were just walking out of Our Lady of Fatima Catholic School. Miriam was almost thirteen, Joseph was eleven, and John Paul was nine and a half. There were only a few days left until Christmas break, and light snowflakes floated to the ground, sticking to the ice-coated sidewalk below. As the children walked out of the building, they were still thinking about what they had learned that day, trying to keep the lessons fresh in their memories. One of the things they remembered was how far Mary and Joseph would've been that day on their journey to Bethlehem, which they kept track of at morning meeting during Advent. Before morning prayer, the principal, Mrs. Anderson, always brought up a big map of Israel in biblical times and pointed to where the Holy Family would travel that day.

Just then, a sudden thought came to Miriam. "Since Mom said she'd pick us up a little later today, why don't we go to the church to pray for a while?" She asked her brothers and sister.

"Why?" John Paul asked hesitantly.

"Just because," Miriam replied, sounding a lot like her mother.

"That sounds like a good idea," Zelie immediately responded. The boys agreed, and the matter was settled.

The Immaculate Heart of Mary parish church wasn't a very long walk for them since it was connected to the school. It looked especially inviting on a frigid day like this.

"We should have just gone through the hallway inside," John Paul mumbled.

"Oh, come on now," said practical, no-nonsense Miriam. "A little fresh air never hurt anyone."

The four children entered the church and genuflected reverently in front of the altar. No one else was in the church, so they knelt down in the first pew. Making the Sign of the Cross, they began to pray.

Candlelight reflected off of the gold Crucifix on the altar. The colorful stained glass windows let the fading winter light into the church. Zelie fingered a silver Rosary Ring she'd discovered in her pocket and started to pray the Divine Mercy Chaplet.

After a few minutes, Father Peters, the parish priest, went up to the altar and replaced a candle that was burning low. Father Peters was an old man with bright blue eyes and thinning white hair. He smiled kindly at the children, then disappeared into the sacristy.

Silence reigned in the church. Then, all of a sudden, Zelie pointed to a part of the church under the statue of the Blessed Virgin Mary. "What's that?" she whispered, jumping up from the kneeler excitedly.

"Shh," Miriam scolded, pressing a finger to her lips. "Don't point in church."

"Why not?" Zelie wondered out loud.

"Because it's rude," Joseph piped up.

John Paul followed Zelie's finger to the wall by the statue. His eyes widened at what he saw.

"Look at that!" He whispered. Now Joseph and Miriam were looking, too. There, underneath the statue, was a carved wooden door. Intricate patterns, leaves, and flowers adorned the solid wood. In the middle of the door, a cross stood out among the other decorations.

"What's that?" Joseph asked, reminding everyone of Zelie's unanswered question.

"Let's go look," John Paul suggested. The four folded up the dark blue, cushiony kneelers and walked over to the altar. They genuflected in front of the tabernacle, then continued to walk towards the mysterious door.

Miriam checked her watch. Their mom wouldn't be there for another fifteen minutes, at least, she figured. She put her hand on the door, a little afraid to open it. "I wonder what's inside," Zelie said.

Chapter 2

Zelie was the first one through the door. Zelie was energetic and bubbly, and she was always quick on her feet. So, it was really no surprise that she was the first to go in. She slipped through the door as quickly and silently as a mouse. You could sense the awe in Zelie's voice as she called to her brothers and sister.

"Guys!" She almost shouted. "Look what I found!"

The other three children rushed into the room. As soon as they saw what was inside, their jaws dropped because of what lay before them. They were speechless. Even Miriam had nothing to say this time, and she *always* had some kind of sensible, informative comment to make.

They realized that the room was a chapel. Three rows of small pews ran through the middle of the room. A wooden altar rail carved with the same intricate designs as the door was positioned in front of the altar. Small statues of Mary and St. Joseph stood in two cut-outs in the wall on either side of the altar. Stained glass windows, miniature versions of the windows inside the church, were built into each wall, giving the chapel an ethereal feeling. Two angels painted in soft colors knelt facing the crucifix in the center of the room.

All throughout the chapel, on every wall, were shelves full of relics. They were all different sizes, shapes, and colors. The children simply stood in the doorway, trying to make sense of their new discovery. They didn't know what to look at first!

John Paul wandered over to a large reliquary in one of the corners. The others followed. The ornate reliquary was made of gold. Blue jewels adorned the reliquary. Two golden angels knelt facing the reliquary between them. Inside the reliquary was a large, antiquated piece of cloth.

Joseph squinted at the small inscription on the plaque in front of the reliquary. "The Sancta Camisia," he read.

"Hey!" John Paul exclaimed. "We learned about that a few days ago in religion class."

"It's the Blessed Virgin Mary's veil, the one she wore when Baby Jesus was born," Miriam supplied. She pressed her fingers to the glass lovingly.

"I thought it was stored in a cathedral in France," Joseph said.

The children stared at each other, deep in thought. How could the Sancta Camisia be here, in a church in their small town, when it was supposed to be in France? How did the rest of the relics get here? It didn't add up. The children hadn't pondered on it for very long, when a shimmery light enveloped them and caused them to look up.

The light swirled around them and grew brighter by the second. Soon, everything around them had disappeared. The last thing Miriam saw was her watch, which read 3:45 p.m. All they could see was the bright light.

Chapter 3

The light gradually faded, then disappeared all together. When she could see again, Miriam realized right away that she wasn't in the chapel anymore. She was all alone; her siblings were nowhere to be seen. Surveying the land around her, she saw that it was dry and bare. *It must be winter here, too,* she thought. The air around her was frigid. When she reached out to pull her school uniform jacket more tightly around her, she didn't feel the familiar blue plush fabric.

In shock, she looked down at her clothing. Her watch, jacket, uniform and sneakers were gone, and her brown scapular no longer hung around her neck. In their place, she was wearing a type of undershirt. On top of that was a shapeless brown tunic. To hold them in place, a pale-blue linen belt was tied around her waist. As a substitute for a jacket, a navy-blue, blanket-like garment was draped over her shoulders. Miriam pulled it tighter around her body, grateful for the little bit of warmth it provided.

She poked her right foot out from under her dress. Looking down at her feet, Miriam noticed that she was wearing leather sandals. Although they weren't as comfortable as her sneakers, they weren't really uncomfortable, either. Her long, dark brown hair was hanging down in a braid that fell past her shoulders, instead of in the usual ponytail pulled back by a scrunchie. Her hair was covered by a cream linen veil.

Casting her gaze from side to side, she looked again for her brothers and sister. No one was around. But out of the corner of her eye, she caught sight of a tall, looming structure in the distance. She turned her head. *A city!* Sure enough, a group of buildings stood to Miriam's left.

Maybe I'll find Joseph, John Paul, and Zelie! she thought. The thought of finding her siblings gave Miriam energy she hadn't realized she needed. She began to sprint for the city. She stopped when she had a stitch in her side. But by then, the city was only a short distance away.

She passed through large gates. Inside the city, the sounds of animals mixed with all sorts of talk created a noisy din.

People milled about, some with animals, some without. Some had bags in hand, some did not. Miriam noticed that all of them dressed in the same style of clothing, similar to what she was wearing. She didn't know where to begin looking for her siblings.

Miriam wandered through the town. She stopped at the busiest area she had seen since her arrival. She saw that, had it been completely empty, the space would have been quite large. Many booths were crowded in, with colorful items displayed at each one. The aroma of spices hit her full-force as she walked towards the market.

At the entrance to the market, a tall man counted fresh-caught fish. Some people were walking around wearing strings of produce around their shoulders. Most of them had the same blanket-like cloaks on, so Miriam figured they were probably like these people's winter coats. They would certainly need something like that; the wind bit through Miriam with a vengeance. A mother, holding a toddler's hand and cradling a baby with her other arm, bought groceries at various booths. Some animals walked around, seemingly unaware that most of them were in the way of the shoppers.

"Goodness," Miriam thought. *"How will I ever find them?"*

Miriam had a good reason to think that way. The market was crowded. Some of the people who ran the

booths seemed a bit overwhelmed with all the customers. But in the distance, she heard a bubbly giggle
that she would recognize anywhere. All she had to do
was follow the sound.

Chapter 4

The shimmering light disappeared. John Paul no longer found himself in between his three siblings, but out on a lonely plain. He turned around and found a gate in front of him. At the entrance to whatever was inside the gate, a gruff-looking man scowled at the ground, then at the hills surrounding the area.

He was an older man, with white hair and a white beard. He was dressed in a dark green tunic, with tan pants. He wore brown leather sandals on his feet. It was nighttime, so he held a lantern bright enough to see anyone who might come to the gate. He leaned on a sturdy wooden staff with his other arm. His face wore a seemingly permanent expression that made the man look as if he had forgotten how to smile.

The man took no notice of John Paul. The boy decided that the mysterious man hadn't noticed him yet. For that was what he was: mysterious. He stared at the ground as if it were the most interesting thing in the world. John Paul wondered if he was trying to count the blades of drying grass below his feet.

A chilly breeze blew through the air. Frost gnawed at the icy green stems poking out of the ground. John Paul immediately decided that he was freezing. He wondered where he was, and when he'd get to go inside. The cloud that had been covering the moon blew across the sky. Moonlight flooded the hilly land.

The sudden breeze and the moon, now shining its light down on them, seemed to stir the older man into a reverie. For a moment, the scowl that John Paul thought was always on his face changed into an awed expression. Peace seemed to fill his being.

"He can't be that bad," John Paul thought to himself.

When he tilted his head and caught sight of John Paul, the man jerked back into reality. He scowled at him.

"You must be the new apprentice," he barked. "Get to your post."

John Paul didn't know what to do. He just nodded and walked quickly to the other side of the gate's entrance, opposite the man. The man seemed satisfied with John Paul's response. *Apprentice? For what?* John Paul wondered. He tried to stifle a yawn. He was exhausted and wondered what he could possibly learn from this crabby old man. How to daydream and scowl? There wasn't another soul in sight.

John Paul sighed. He could tell that this was going to be a *long* night. All he wanted to do was crawl into bed. That's where he wanted to be. That's where he should be. As these thoughts ran through his mind, he sighed again.

A soft light glowed on the shadowy path leading to John Paul and the man. The man lifted his staff and lantern. John Paul followed the light with his eyes. The light came steadily closer, and John Paul made out the figures of two people and an animal. One person was riding on the animal, while the other led them along, holding a staff.

Pretty soon, the couple was standing in front of the man and John Paul. The man was leading the donkey, gripping on tightly to the reins. On the donkey's back was a beautiful woman dressed in a white gown and a blue mantle.

"We're here for the census," the man holding the reins said. But the man John Paul had been standing outside of the gate with hardly heard him. For at that moment, the woman lifted her head and gazed at the older man. His whole being changed. As the lady smiled at him with her soft, loving eyes, he was no longer harsh and gruff.

A smile softened the man's face. "I'll take you to the inn," he told the couple.

He pulled open the large gate and led them through the tall, stone structure. The lady greeted John Paul with a friendly smile as she rode past. John Paul watched them get smaller and smaller in the distance, until they were no bigger than a speck. They rounded a corner and were gone.

John Paul turned his attention to the beautiful night. The moonlight seemed heavenly, and the stars shone brighter than John Paul had ever seen.

The man came back and resumed his post. He cast his glance at John Paul, and said, "My name's Mordecai." Motioning towards the city inside the gate he said, "I'm the night watchman here in Bethlehem."

Chapter 5

Miriam found Zelie sitting in front of a fruit stand with two other girls about the same age as she was. Miriam smiled to herself. Leave it to Zelie to make friends as soon as she arrived in a new place.

"Miriam!!" Zelie exclaimed when she saw her big sister. She flung herself at Miriam and wrapped her arms around her. Miriam hugged her back. Spinning around to face the girls she'd been sitting next to, she introduced them.

Pointing towards the older girl, Zelie said, "This is Junia." Then, pointing to the younger one, she said, "And this is Eve."

Junia had thick, dark brown hair that was neatly covered by a veil. Her younger sister had similar facial features and hair that was just slightly lighter than Junia's. Her hair was also covered by a veil, but not very neatly.

"Nice to meet you," Miriam said politely. She smiled at her sister's new friends.

"I've been hanging out with them since I got here," Zelie said. The other girls seemed a little puzzled at Zelie's expression but didn't question what "hanging out" meant. "They help their parents at the stand." Miriam nodded attentively.

A man and a woman stood behind the stand. The man had Junia's dark brown locks, while his wife's hair was a little lighter than Eve's. Like their daughters, they were of medium height. From the way they interacted with the customers, they seemed to be kind, honest, and hard-working people.

For most of the day, Miriam and Zelie stayed at the family's fruit stand in the market. They helped with the many customers who came to the stand. The family shared their meals with them, and in between, the girls chatted as if they had been best friends for years. Their meals consisted of bread, dried fish, and fruit that Junia and Eve's parents were selling.

Although most of the women in the marketplace just wore veils, others wore hairnets, and some wore both. Then there were some who didn't wear a head covering at all. Most of the women wore their hair braided like Junia, Eve, Zelie, and Miriam. As for the rest of their outfits, their tunics or dresses were similar to what Miriam and Zelie were wearing.

About fifteen minutes into the conversation, Junia turned to Miriam and asked the question Miriam dreaded answering.

"Where are you from?"

Do something, Zelie, Miriam silently pleaded. Zelie thought hard.

"We're, um," Miriam stammered. She couldn't seem to answer the question – she didn't even know where she was now!

"We're from a farm a few hours away from here," Zelie interrupted. Miriam released the breath she hadn't known she was holding. She silently thanked God for giving her a smart little sister who could always get her out of a jam.

"That's right," Miriam continued. "Our parents are farmers, and we're staying with some relatives who live outside of town."

Junia and Eve didn't seem to notice anything too fishy and went on to another topic with Zelie. As soon as their backs were turned, Miriam cringed at the stupid, made-up story. Mr. and Mrs. Langford being farmers was about as far from the truth as you could get. Their father was the religion teacher for grades 3-6 at the kids' school, and their mother worked at the museum, setting up exhibits and helping with school field trips to the museum. Mrs. Langford also ran a monthly book club for adults at the library.

The children had always thought that their parents' jobs were the best jobs ever. Sometimes, when Mr. Langford brought the kids home after school, they got to hang out in his classroom while he went to the teachers' meetings or finished packing up his things. He had all sorts of cool things, from board games of all kinds to the 64-pack set of Crayola broad-tip markers, and he always let them draw little pictures in the margins of his whiteboard. Their mother's job was equally entertaining, as it resulted in lots of extra trips to the museum. Once, Mrs. Langford showed them the rooms where all of the things that weren't currently on display were stored, letting the children "ooh" and "ah" over each item with an enthusiastic smile on her face. The Langfords also made regular trips to the town's library. All of the Langford children were avid readers, and their parents enjoyed a good book every now and then, too.

Miriam reminded herself that she and Zelie would have to go to confession as soon as they got home so that they could confess their lie – if they got home. She shuddered at the horrifying possibility.

A short woman with bright auburn hair walked through the marketplace, carrying a large basket full of groceries. Her hair wasn't braided but framed her face and fell just above her shoulders. She didn't wear a veil, either. Her green eyes had a warmth to them that matched her smile perfectly, making everyone feel right at home. She waved at them, smiling.

"Hi, Elisabeth!" Junia greeted the woman.

"These are our new friends, Miriam and Zelie," Eve added.

"Nice to meet you girls," Elisabeth said before continuing out of the market.

"Who was that?" Miriam asked Junia.

"That's Elisabeth. She's the innkeeper's wife. She's also a friend of ours."

When evening came, Miriam said, "We'd better get going."

"Bye, Junia!" Zelie called. "Bye, Eve!"

"Goodbye!" They called.

Miriam and Zelie walked out of the marketplace. "Where are we going, Miriam?" Zelie asked, lowering her voice a bit so that only her big sister could hear.

"I don't know," Miriam replied uncertainly. "We'll figure something out." It wasn't like Miriam actually believed that. But she wasn't going to let Zelie know about the fears that were roaring inside of her. No, she would keep calm and try to figure something out like she'd promised her little sister. *Think, Miriam*, she pleaded with herself.

Up ahead, a sign read, "INN". Miriam quickened her pace and pulled Zelie along. "Look! Maybe we can stay there!" She exclaimed.

A woman, dressed in blue, was sitting on a donkey outside of the inn. A boy, who Miriam supposed was probably her son, patiently held her possessions. A tall man was standing on the doorstep, asking if he and his wife could stay the night. They looked cold and tired.

"Please," they heard him say. "My wife is having a baby very soon." The innkeeper was silent for a moment, deep in thought.

"I know it isn't much," he said, "but you can stay in a stable that I own." He gave them the directions, and the couple happily went down the road.

Timidly, the girls approached the innkeeper. He wasn't a short man, but he wasn't tall, either. He was a little shorter than their father.

"Hi," Miriam said. "We'd like a place to sleep for the night."

The innkeeper, sympathy spreading across his face, said, "I'm sorry, but I'm all out of rooms." He rubbed his temples like he had a headache.

"Oh, that's alright." Miriam told him. They turned to leave. As they walked through the moonlit streets, the stars shone brightly. Especially one bright star, just a little ways off in the distance. It seemed so close to the earth; Miriam thought for a minute that she could touch it if she only jumped high enough.

"You know," Zelie said, "I think we might be in Bethlehem."

"I don't know," Miriam replied, wishing she knew exactly what was going on. The girls walked in silence for a while. Then, Miriam asked her little sister, "How did you get here?"

"You know that bright light that was in the chapel?" Miriam nodded. "Well," Zelie continued, "That got so bright, I couldn't see anymore. Then, when the light disappeared, I was at the entrance to the market, dressed like this." She pointed to the clothes she was wearing – a navy blue tunic with a brown belt and a brown cloak. Her hair was covered by a white veil. "That's when I met Junia and Eve."

"That's pretty much the same thing that happened to me," Miriam told her sister, "except when the light disappeared, I was outside the city. Then I came here, hoping to find you and the boys."

"I wonder where the boys are now," Zelie worried.

"I'm sure they're fine," Miriam said, trying to comfort her little sister. She reached for Zelie's hand, entwining her fingers with Zelie's. "We'll look for them tomorrow."

But she wasn't so sure of that herself.

The girls found an old building that looked like it had once been a shed of some sort. There was still hay on the ground, and water troughs were spread unevenly throughout the space. Wooden planks were scattered throughout the building, some of which looked like they'd fallen off the building's structure. Miriam rearranged some of the hay, and she and Zelie cuddled up in the corner. Zelie fell asleep as soon as she lay against the wall. She had had a big day.

But Miriam couldn't sleep. Worries filled her mind. She worried about where Joseph and John Paul were, and if they'd ever get back home all in one piece. The fact that the old building looked about ready to cave in on them didn't help her nerves any.

Sharp pieces of hay prickled against her back, and she was certain she'd be picking hay out of her hair for weeks if not months. She tried to extinguish the thoughts and focus on something else.

Turning to Zelie, she noticed that she was shivering. Miriam wrapped her mantle around Zelie. After a while, Miriam drifted off to sleep.

Elisabeth walked through the marketplace, balancing a heavy basket of groceries on her arm.

"How are you and Thaddeus doing?" One of her friends, Rebekah, popped out of nowhere with her little girl and new baby boy.

"We're fine!" Elisabeth exclaimed, happy to see her friend. "The inn's busy, as usual. How are you and Jacob?"

Elisabeth was married to Thaddeus, the innkeeper in Bethlehem. Ever since Caesar Augustus decreed that a census should be taken, people had been flocking to Bethlehem left and right. If any more people came just that day, Thaddeus and Elisabeth would be completely out of room.

"Oh, we're doing well," Rebekah told Elisabeth. She tucked a loose strand of pale brown hair into her linen veil and shifted the baby in her arms. Both women turned when they heard another traveler knock on the inn's heavy door.

"I'd better get back home now," Elisabeth said apologetically, glancing towards the inn. "Now that it's almost suppertime, more people will arrive soon, and I still have to cook supper!"

"Tell Thaddeus that Jacob says hello," Rebekah replied, picking up her grocery basket.

"I will."

Elisabeth walked towards the inn, waving at Hannah and Aaron, another couple of Thaddeus and Elisabeth's friends. She smiled down at their two girls, Junia and Eve, who were talking to two girls Elisabeth had never seen before. Something seemed different about them; Elisabeth just couldn't quite put a finger on it. She decided that they were probably there for the census, just like many other strangers walking the streets of Bethlehem.

"Hi, Elisabeth!" Junia called.

"These are our new friends, Miriam and Zelie," Eve added.

"Nice to meet you girls," Elisabeth said cordially.

She continued to walk out of the marketplace, setting her basket down in the small courtyard outside of the inn. Pushing her bright auburn, shoulder-length hair behind her ear, she started a fire and went to fill up a jar with water. When she got back from the well that stood in the center of the town, she poured the water into the pot and added meat and vegetables to make a broth. The fire warmed her up quickly after walking around in the freezing-cold marketplace.

Another visitor came. Thaddeus helped them inside. After two more visitors had gone in, Elisabeth carried in different bowls for the meal. This was her favorite part of the day – serving guests and making them feel like part of her own family.

That night, she went to bed, thinking about the new guests and what she could do to help them until she fell asleep. However, Thaddeus didn't sleep as peacefully. He tossed and turned, worrying that more guests would come. He and Elisabeth both knew that they were completely out of room.

Later that evening, Elisabeth woke up, worrying about her husband. She couldn't sleep; she was just as restless as Thaddeus. Just then, Thaddeus was awoken by a knock at the door. Elisabeth draped a dark green shawl around her shoulders and quickly lit a lantern. Thaddeus got out of bed and opened the door.

Elisabeth's heart went out to the couple who stood outside the door; they looked so cold and tired. From a glance at Thaddeus's face, she could tell he was thinking the same thing. Felix, a fourteen-year-old boy who didn't live far from the inn, stood behind the couple, holding two small bags.

The woman was the most beautiful person Elisabeth had ever seen. She was dressed in blue, with a creamy-white veil. Dark brown locks framed her exquisite face. Her blue eyes shone in the darkness from beneath her veil. She sat on top of a donkey.

Her husband was tall with a sturdy build. His muscles protruded from beneath his cloak. He carried a staff and held the donkey's rope. He had a rough brown beard and thick brown hair.

"Please," the man said to them, concern filling his dark brown eyes. "My wife is having a baby very soon."

Elisabeth couldn't think of a way to help the couple, but she held on to the hope that Thaddeus would think of another option. He stared out into the night, lost in thought.

"I know it isn't much, but you could stay in a stable that I own," he told the travelers. "It's a little ways

out of town." He finished giving them directions, and they gladly went on their way.

"I wish there was something more we could do to help them," Elisabeth told her husband as he closed the door and latched it shut.

"I know," he said. "We'll get up early tomorrow and try to make them a little more comfortable. Maybe there will be an open room."

Thaddeus went back to bed. But Elisabeth stayed up a while longer, thinking about the couple and their new baby. Realizing that there was nothing she could do until the next morning, she blew out the lamp.

Chapter 6

Joseph felt like he had just come out of a dream. He felt dazed when the dazzling light vanished. He found himself in a large, grassy area. Rocks dotted the plain, and he felt even more confused when a sheep ran just in front of his feet.

A shepherd ran after the little renegade, taking little notice of Joseph. Joseph, not knowing where he was or what to do, wandered over to a pile of rocks and sat down. A woman was sitting down near him, turning a stick-like object with thread attached in her hands.

Never pausing her work, she looked up at Joseph and smiled. "Would you like some water?" she asked, motioning towards a jar near her. Joseph nodded gratefully. Maybe it would help to clear his head.

Other people that Joseph had seen with the sheep earlier started to head towards a fire with a pot over it. Joseph decided that was probably where he needed to be, too. The woman set aside her tools and followed him to the site. All of the people there were dressed in a style of clothing that Joseph had never seen people wearing before. He was shocked to discover that he was wearing those clothes, too!

31

Most of the people were men, but there were some women and girls there, too. The woman behind Joseph quickly walked in front of him to join the other women. She started helping them serve the meal. Joseph decided it must be suppertime, looking at how low the sun was setting in the sky.

A plate of bread and meat was set before Joseph. He thanked the lady who gave it to him as she walked by, passing out food. When he turned his head, he recognized who was sitting next to him. It was the boy who had been chasing the runaway lamb!

The boy recognized Joseph. Then they both started laughing. It was most likely due to the fact that they kept bumping into each other but didn't know who the other was!

The boy started the introductions. "I'm Silas," he told Joseph. Joseph introduced himself. Then Silas introduced his family.

"That's my mother, Ruth," Silas said, pointing out the woman who had offered Joseph a drink. He then pointed out his father and brother, along with a few other shepherds.

When the evening sky began to darken and the stars came out, Joseph walked with Silas and the other shepherds who would be watching the sheep during the night.

"Tonight, we get to stay up with Mark," Silas whispered to Joseph. "He tells the best stories."

Mark sat down beside the fire. The flames quickly warmed up the shepherds as the wind whipped around them, chilling anyone it touched. Joseph and Silas sat down beside him. As the other shepherds came towards the fire, Joseph remarked to Silas, "Wow. The stars sure are beautiful tonight."

"Yes, they are," replied Silas. "But I wonder why that one star is there. I've never seen it before."

Silas was pointing up to a star, bigger than all of the others. It was brighter than all the rest, too. No one knew why it was there, but they marveled at its beauty. The star seemed to want people to notice it.

The boys leaned against a rock and waited for Mark to begin his story. Suddenly, a bright, almost blinding flash of light made everyone look up. The light dimmed a little so that the shepherds could see an angel walk out. The shepherds jumped; they were startled and scared. The angel spoke to them.

"Do not be afraid; for behold, I proclaim to you good news of great joy that will be for all the people. For today in the city of David a savior has been born for you who is Messiah and Lord. And this will be a sign for you: you will find an infant wrapped in swaddling clothes and lying in a manger."

When the angel had finished speaking, many other angels appeared. They praised God and sang a melody that reminded Joseph of the Gloria they sang at Mass.

"Glory to God in the highest, and on earth peace to those on whom his favor rests," the angels sang.

Then they disappeared into the night as quickly as they had come.

Mark looked at another older shepherd and said two words: "Let's go." The other shepherd nodded and went to spread the good news to the others.

Chapter 7

The sun was just barely up when Zelie woke to the sound of animals walking around outside of the building. "Miriam!" Zelie said as loudly as she dared. "Wake up!" She lightly tapped Miriam on the shoulder.

Her older sister yawned and started to slowly sit up. "Can we go find the boys yet?" Zelie asked excitedly.

"Not yet," Miriam replied with a smile. "I think we should go check in with Junia and Eve at the marketplace first. Otherwise, they might wonder what happened to us."

Zelie made no protest, and together the girls walked through the city streets. Miriam could tell that today was going to be warmer. There was hardly any wind at all.

The girls had no trouble finding the marketplace. This was partly due to the fact that it was fairly close to their temporary abode, and partly due to the fact that you could hear the market a mile away.

Zelie found Junia and Eve at their parents' stand. The two girls had been up and at 'em since sunrise, helping the early risers who came to the market. They told Miriam and Zelie that while most came in the late morning or afternoon, some wanted to get their shopping over with as soon as possible.

Miriam and Zelie ate breakfast and lunch with the girls. Their morning schedule was almost identical to their schedule from the day before, but this time, Miriam had a different after-lunch activity planned.

Miriam hadn't been there for very long, but she already loved the market. She loved the sights, the sounds of animals and people talking, and the smells of the fresh fruits and vegetables that had just been taken to the booths. The market reminded Miriam of the mall back home in Woodrift, a place she'd always liked to go shopping. The thought brought back special memories of going there with her mom, Zelie, and sometimes her friends from school.

After lunch, Miriam rose to leave. Miriam told Junia and Eve that she and Zelie had some other errands to run. Zelie got up, and the sisters said goodbye to Junia and Eve. Zelie, always ready for an adventure, followed her older sister out of the market.

Zelie could hardly contain her excitement. They were going to try to find the boys! Maybe, if they found them, they could answer all of Zelie's questions that she'd been curious about since her arrival. *Did you get out of the shimmering light when you got here? Did you see that big, pretty star? Do you know where we are? Where have you been?*

Although it was wintertime, the sky was clear as the girls walked out of the marketplace. Well, Miriam walked, at least. Zelie practically flew. But that was just like Zelie – always full of excitement.

Miriam had carefully planned their adventure. They started at the market since it was located at the heart of the city. Since it was also the busiest place, it seemed like the perfect spot to find someone. They would continue through the main street to the other side of the city, and if they still hadn't found anyone, they would explore every other place the boys could possibly be within the city. Miriam hoped her plan would work efficiently; she wanted to cover as much ground as she could. She knew that it would be hard to find someone after dark, so they only had a few hours of precious daylight left.

They took a left turn, the direction opposite of the man who counted fish and other goods being brought to the market for sale. They passed a few buildings, and then an area that looked like a court-yard in the middle of the city. A large well stood up straight in the middle of the courtyard, and flocks of women gathered around the large structure. All had jars in hand. While a few were dipping their jars into the well, most of them were standing around, chatting while their jars sat on the ground beside them.

The girls continued on to the gate at the other side of the city. This was the other entrance, not the one Miriam had entered the city through. It was still hard to see if anyone was over there, as the girls were still a good distance away. But when they got closer, they made out the figures of two people.

"JOHN PAUL!!!" Zelie squealed at the top of her lungs. She ran towards one of the people at full force. One of them caught her before she could tumble down the hill. She hugged that person tightly, making it clear who had caught her. When Miriam got closer, she saw that it was indeed John Paul.

Miriam greeted John Paul. She was enthusiastic about it, just not quite as enthusiastic as Zelie was. It wasn't that she wasn't happy to see her brother, it was just that she didn't have all of Zelie's energy.

They sat down next to John Paul, and questions started pouring out of Zelie's mouth. "Whoa," John Paul said. "One question at a time."

"Okay," Zelie told him. "What are you doing here?"

"I'm the watchman's apprentice here in Bethlehem."

"I knew it!" Zelie exclaimed with vigor, pumping her fist in the air. "I knew we were in Bethlehem!"

But Miriam was puzzled. "Watchman's apprentice?" she asked John Paul. He gave his sister a look that said *I'll tell you later.* For at that moment, a medium-sized man with a snowy beard walked towards them.

"This is Mordecai," John Paul told the girls. "These are my sisters, Miriam and Zelie," he then said to Mordecai. Mordecai nodded and smiled at Miriam and Zelie. Then he walked back to the other side of the gate and continued to watch the road as he leaned on his wooden staff.

Chapter 8

The next morning, around fifteen shepherds gathered in the center of the campsite. Many came with small bags of supplies and water. Silas's mother carried a lovely blanket.

Ruth walked over to the boys and handed each of them two small bags. She explained that one held water, and the other held food. The boys thanked her and went to join the other shepherds.

Most of the sheep were staying in the camp, and the rest of the shepherds would stay with them. But a few sheep would come with the shepherds who were going to find the Messiah. They were going to give one of the best lambs to him.

They set out on their journey as the sun was just coming up, streaking the sky with pink, purple and orange hues. For a while, they walked through open patches of grass. A stream ran through the side of one of the fields. Silas told Joseph that it was the same one they got their water from.

Silas and Joseph eventually fell behind the rest of the shepherds but decided that it was alright. They weren't in a huge hurry, anyway. They were just enjoying themselves, like any two friends would do.

They talked, ran, and sometimes lingered behind to examine a plant or insect that interested them. Before they knew it, the sun was starting to sink towards the horizon.

The grown-ups took a turn and followed the leaders of the group into a dense forest. The boys hurried up because they realized they were too far back. But when they got into the forest, they realized that it was too late. The grown-ups were gone.

The forest was a dark place – the type of place that you have to tip-toe in so as not to disturb its slumber. Silvery spiderwebs hung on the branches of tall trees that stretched towards the sky, their branches creating leafy canopies over the forest. "Oh no," Joseph almost whispered.

"We'll be alright," Silas responded. "Let's go this way."

He pointed to the right. Joseph followed him, deciding that, having lived here all his life, Silas probably knew more about the forest than he did. They hadn't walked very far in that direction when Silas almost squeaked, "We're lost."

Joseph didn't know what to do. He was afraid and a little upset at himself for listening to Silas. "Let's just keep going," Joseph suggested, trying to keep calm as panic built inside of him. "Maybe we'll find our way out."

They kept going. The trees got thicker and closer together. Joseph tripped over the roots of a large tree. By then, all of the trees and bushes were so close together that there was barely any room to walk. Silas and Joseph sat down, discouraged.

Silas sighed loudly and leaned against the trunk of a tree. It seemed like he'd given up already. *We have to get out of here. But how?*" The question replayed, over and over, inside Joseph's brain. Joseph stared up at the little bit of sky that was visible through the thick leaves and branches of the trees, trying to think of a solution.

The star! Suddenly, Joseph knew what to do. They should follow the star! He tapped Silas on the arm and told him his plan. They got up and started pushing their way through the branches that scratched and snapped at their faces and arms.

After a few minutes, the path started to widen. Soon, everything was bathed in the silver moonlight.

Joseph and Silas were out of the woods! They could see a city in the distance. The star was just over the city. The boys began to sprint, running towards the star.

Morning light had just barely started to illuminate the room when Thaddeus gently shook his wife awake. Elisabeth noticed right away that he was fully dressed and ready to start the day.

"I wonder if the Child was born last night," Thaddeus remarked.

"Let's go see if they need anything," Elisabeth responded. "Maybe we should bring them some supplies, to help make their stay more comfortable."

She put on her shawl and sandals. Thaddeus opened the door as Elisabeth lit her lantern, and together the couple walked out into the street. Not a single soul was walking around – an unusual sight with everyone in town for the census. Not even the market was awake.

"I hope they aren't asleep," Elisabeth worried. "I don't want to wake them up."

"No, I don't think we will," replied her husband, trying to calm her nerves.

Elisabeth clutched a hefty bundle of blankets in her arms. She would have liked to take more, but their arms were completely full. Thaddeus was carrying a basket of bread and vegetables in one hand, and he grasped the handle of a jar of water with his other. Just then, Elisabeth spotted Felix walking through the streets.

She waved him over and asked him if he would help them carry some other items. He eagerly agreed. Elisabeth handed him the blankets she held and went back to the inn, careful not to wake the travelers. She carefully took baby clothes and the cradle that had once held their son, long tucked away.

Tears sprung to her eyes as she thought of Adam, the happy baby boy whose life had been taken by fever. She pushed all unpleasant thoughts out of her mind, reminding herself that there would soon be a new baby, which was a happy occasion.

Felix and Thaddeus were waiting outside. She handed the wooden cradle to Felix, who took it carefully, understanding whose it had been. Thaddeus looked at Elisabeth, his gaze betraying his sadness. He looked away, turning his eyes to the city. Elisabeth picked up her blankets and lantern, and they walked through the city with Felix.

When they arrived at the stable, Elisabeth almost fell back a step out of her wonder and amazement. The sight she witnessed warmed her heart. There, in the middle of the stable, was a manger glowing with light from the special baby inside. His mother and father knelt nearby, perfect joy and peace on their faces. Elisabeth felt a heavenly joy inside of her, her heart beating faster as she approached the family.

"The Messiah," she heard Felix whisper as he stared at the Baby in wonder.

Joseph hesitated a moment, but looking back at Mary, he nodded, confirming Felix's realization.

Felix, Thaddeus, and Elisabeth knelt down in front of the newborn king. Elisabeth lovingly gazed down at His perfect face. After a moment, His mother, Mary, gently picked the Baby up. Smiling, she laid Him in Elisabeth's arms.

"His name is Jesus," Joseph told them. Elisabeth stared down in wonder, holding Baby Jesus close to her. She closed her eyes, letting it all sink in. Several of the most wonderful minutes of her life had passed

when Elisabeth realized she should give Baby Jesus back to Mary. Mary took Him, her face radiant.

Elisabeth offered the family their gifts, but they wouldn't accept the cradle or the baby clothes. "They are yours," Mary said, placing them back in Elisabeth's arms. "You will need them."

Elisabeth questioned what Mary had said, but never came to a good conclusion. She didn't have time to think about it, so she pushed the thought to the back of her mind.

Felix soon had to go back to the marketplace, but Elisabeth and Thaddeus stayed as long as they possibly could. When it came time for them to go, Elisabeth felt like she couldn't leave.

"Thank you so much," she told the Holy Family.

"We'll come back tomorrow to see if you need anything," Thaddeus added.

Joseph and Mary smiled up at them. Together, Elisabeth and Thaddeus left, joy filling their hearts for the rest of the day.

Chapter 9

"Will he let you come with us?" Miriam asked John Paul.

"I don't know," replied John Paul uncertainly, glancing back at the older watchman. "I'll go check."

John Paul trotted across the path to where Mordecai stood. Miriam and Zelie saw John Paul talking to the older man, asking his question. Mordecai nodded, then smiled at the girls to let them know it was okay.

John Paul ran back over to the girls, and together, they walked through the main city street. "How in the world did you become an apprentice?" Miriam asked. Never in her life had she imagined studious John Paul would become a watchman's apprentice!

"When I got here, I was at the gate. Mordecai was there, and at first he was really crabby. Now he's better. Anyway, he just told me to go over there and said something about me being the new apprentice. By the way, he said it was okay to come with you."

"Oh," Miriam said. There didn't seem to be much more she could say. But Zelie definitely had things to say!

"Did you see the shiny light, too?" Zelie wanted to know.

"Actually, I did," John Paul replied. "That's when I got here."

"We must be in Bethlehem during the time of Jesus," Zelie decided. "Oh, John Paul, do you want to go meet Junia and Eve?"

"Sure," he told her, shrugging his shoulders. He had no idea who Junia and Eve were, but he didn't want to dampen his little sister's spirits, so he let Zelie lead him along. Miriam nodded her agreement. Together, the three set off for the marketplace. But the unspoken question was on everyone's minds: *Where is Joseph?*

John Paul was stunned – and a little overwhelmed – by the marketplace. All the colors and smells passed by him in a blur. He blindly let Miriam and Zelie lead him along to meet Junia and Eve as he tried to process all he was seeing.

His sisters stopped in front of a booth filled to the brim with colorful pieces of fruit. Several customers were buzzing around the counter, being helped by a man, a woman, and two young girls. The shopkeepers seemed outnumbered by all of the customers.

"This is Junia and Eve's stand!" Zelie exclaimed, eagerly tugging on John Paul's arm. Since she was closest in age to him, she had always had a special affection for her older brother. They had been almost inseparable since the day Zelie was born. Of course, Zelie loved all of her siblings with her signature enthusiasm, but she and John Paul shared a special bond.

Junia caught sight of the three siblings, and her face lit up. She continued to help her parents, but occasionally looked over at Zelie, Miriam, and John Paul. When she got a minute's break, she patted Eve's arm and pointed at their friends. Eve smiled, too.

Finally, after about ten minutes, there was only one customer left. The girls' father helped him, and the girls came over to Miriam, John Paul, and Zelie. After John Paul was introduced (and Junia and Eve welcomed him warmly), the girls began to talk, like they always did when they were together.

Just a couple minutes into their conversation, a tall boy, about Miriam's age, walked up the street. He had curly, reddish-brown hair and a good-natured smile. He was walking with two toddlers – a girl and a boy.

"Then what happened?" The little girl asked excitedly.

"They lived happily ever after," the older boy said.

"The end," the little boy finished for him. Two women came, and the toddlers ran over to them and took their mothers' hands. Miriam heard them telling the women all about their adventures of the day.

The boy approached the children. When he got closer, Miriam realized that he was about the same age as her. He smiled kindly at the little group. Miriam smiled back – partly to return his beaming grin, partly because of his kindness to the toddlers. He loped up to them.

"Felix!" Eve exclaimed. She rose to greet him. Junia greeted him too, and introduced Miriam, John Paul, and Zelie. Miriam could tell he was trying to be polite, but he clearly had something to say, too. Finally, he let it spill out.

"You'll never guess what just happened!" Felix exclaimed. Miriam watched as the girls hung on his every word. Their eyes grew large in their excitement.

Zelie was excited, too. She rocked back and forth until she almost fell over.

When Felix knew they were listening, he told them, "A baby was born last night! He's the Messiah! He's out in Thaddeus's stable, outside of town!"

"That's wonderful!" Junia exclaimed in delight. "Come on, Eve, let's go tell Mama and Papa!"

Felix's good-natured grin spread across his face. "I'm going with my parents right now. You should come!" And with that, he jogged out of the marketplace.

Miriam thought that Felix looked familiar. During their conversation she had been trying to place him, sure that she knew him from somewhere. Suddenly, it dawned on her as she watched Felix exit the market. *Of course!* She thought. *He's the boy who was carrying the bags at the inn!*

Miriam was stirred back into reality when Junia and Eve came running towards the three siblings. Eve grabbed Miriam and Zelie's hands. "Come on!" She exclaimed impatiently. "We're going to see the newborn king!"

Junia and Eve's parents followed their daughters. Together, they almost ran out of the market. They were going to see the Messiah!

Chapter 10

Miriam, filled with excitement and joy, didn't have a doubt in her mind now that they were in Bethlehem. She felt completely at peace. Miriam knew that wherever Joseph was God would take care of him, just like He did for her, Zelie, and John Paul. Her heart felt so light, she felt like she could fly!

Miriam hummed a tune she had heard at Mass a couple of times.

Soon and very soon, we are going to see the King!
Soon and very soon, we are going to see the King!
Soon and very soon, we are going to see the King.
Alleluia, Alleluia! We're going to see the King!

Other people who lived in Bethlehem were heading in the same direction. *They must be going to see Jesus, too,* Miriam thought. Her joy surpassed all of the worries she'd had in the past two days. *This,* Miriam was sure, *is one of the best days of my life.*

"There it is!" Silas said, pointing to a tall stone gate in the distance. When Joseph saw the city, he became hopeful once more that he would find his siblings. The last day and a half had been a whirlwind for him.

It had started with his arrival in the shepherds' camp without his siblings. He had made a new friend. He had met and helped shepherds. He had seen angels and a star, and he had gotten lost in a thick forest.

Joseph recounted his adventures, especially his and Silas's trials in the forest. When they got out of the forest after following the star, the rest of the shepherds were there, about to go in and search for them. Ruth embraced Silas, and after she let him go, she shook her head at the bruises and scrapes covering the boys' arms. She reprimanded her son and his friend for not following the group, but the scolding was somewhat gentle. Relief was present on her face when she hugged Silas again.

They heard the whole story from Mark on the way to Bethlehem. By then, the boys had a story to tell Mark, too. Ruth was sick with worry about them, Mark told them. He said that when she discovered that the boys were missing, she dropped everything she was carrying and ran to tell the leader of the party that they needed to go look for the boys. Everyone began to retrace their steps, which led them back to the forest.

In return, the boys told Mark the story of how they had gotten lost in the forest, and how the star had led them out.

Joseph gasped. Never in his life had he seen such a thing. He stopped and stared, his jaw dropping open.

It was a magnificent, enormous gate, made completely out of stone. It was so tall, Joseph could barely tell where the top of it met the sky. A large gate stood tall and proud in the middle of the wall.

"I think there's supposed to be a watchman to let us in," Mark told the boys. He motioned to the leaders' confused faces. Finally, one of the leaders motioned towards the other shepherds to follow while the other pulled open the gate. Joseph figured it must be heavy, for it looked like the shepherd put a lot of effort into his task.

Ruth gathered up her things, which she had temporarily set down. The shepherds flooded through the gates and into the little town of Bethlehem.

If the night hadn't been illuminated by thousands of bright stars and the soft yet powerful moonlight, the buildings would have blended into the darkness. There wasn't a single light on in the city. Usually, in their house, it was "lights out," but there was always one house in their neighborhood that kept the lights on late into the night. Here, all of the houses' windows were pitch black.

The group wandered down one of the streets. The farther into the town they went, the more Joseph believed that it must be deserted. It looked like one of the ghost towns he'd seen on TV. They rounded a corner and found themselves back at the gate they'd entered the city through. But this time, they noticed something that hadn't been there before. Or maybe they just hadn't noticed it. Whatever it was, it was definitely there now.

"It's the star!" Silas exclaimed. "How did we not notice that before?"

The shepherds at the head of the group were already running towards the hill that seemed to glow in the star's light. It seemed to be directly under the star. It was a long walk across a large field, but if that was where the Messiah was, then they would go.

When they got to their destination, they saw that it was full of people. Most of them looked like villagers from Bethlehem. They were all standing or kneeling in front of a small, worn building. It definitely looked like it was falling apart. But there was a feeling of peace around it. It was completely bathed in light. The source of the light was coming from inside the stable, but Joseph couldn't tell exactly where it was coming from. There were so many people, it was hard to see. He heard a drum beating in a captivating rhythm somewhere near the entrance to the stable.

Joseph felt lost and out of place in the crowd. He didn't know where to go or what to do. As he and the other shepherds approached the small stable, they were separated. The crowd seemed to swallow Joseph up. Dazed, Joseph looked around. He was surrounded on all sides by strangers, who were all trying to push their way closer to the small building.

The crowd shifted again. More people pushed their way to the front of the crowd. Joseph caught sight of a girl a few inches taller than him with dark hair. She turned. Their gaze met. Joseph gasped.

"Miriam," he whispered. Then again, "Miriam!" This time he was more certain. In fact, he was almost positive that this was his older sister. Her expression showed pure shock. She turned the other direction again. The next time she turned, two more people turned towards Joseph with her. *Zelie! John Paul!*

The four siblings were reunited at last. They huddled together in one big group hug. Miriam's smile almost seemed bigger than her face.

By this time, quite a bit of the crowd had dispersed. It was Junia and Eve's family's turn to see Baby Jesus. When they approached the Holy Family, they knelt down in unison. The family glanced at each other and seemed to know just what to say. "We give you our prayers," they said together. Mary smiled up at them. After sitting with the Holy Family for a few more moments, they got up. The girls' mother nodded at the four children to let them know that they could go.

The four children slowly approached the stable. The whole building glowed with Jesus's light. The star's light could never compete with this light. A soft glow surrounded the peaceful, happy family. His Mother smiled up at the children.

Mary was the most beautiful lady that the children had ever seen. Her eyes sparkled in the moonlight. St. Joseph looked caring and kind. He had a brown beard with hair the same dark color, and he knelt beside his family. And Baby Jesus was the most beautiful, most perfect baby there ever was. Small pieces of dark hair covered His tiny head. He lay quietly in the manger, smiling up at the children. There were almost no words to describe the scene that was right in front of the children's eyes.

Speechless, the four siblings knelt side by side. Miriam wondered for a minute if they were actually there. *Yes*, she thought. *Yes, we are in Bethlehem!*

Miriam smiled at her sudden realization. Baby Jesus was right in front of them! Still smiling, Miriam knelt down with her siblings to pray. After a few minutes, the children stood up. Although they wanted to stay longer, to be with Jesus for a few moments more, they got up because they knew that other people wanted to see Jesus, too.

Silas's family went next. Ruth handed her wonderful blanket to Jesus's mother. When Mary said "thank-you", her voice was so soft and so sweet; it sounded like a gentle melody.

After staying a few moments longer and setting the lamb before the manger where Jesus lay, the shepherds prepared to leave. Silas had gathered that Miriam, John Paul, and Zelie were Joseph's siblings.

"Are you coming back with us?" Silas asked Joseph as they walked away from the stable. Joseph looked back at his sisters and brother. They were listening and waiting for Joseph's reply. As he gazed at his siblings, he knew what his answer would be.

Without hesitating, he responded, "I think I'll stay with my siblings."

"Alright," Silas replied. "I'll miss you," he said after a moment.

"I'll miss you, too," Joseph told his friend. "Good-bye."

Silas shuffled towards the other shepherds, who were preparing to leave. Joseph watched the shepherds disappear over the hills of Bethlehem. Then, he turned and ran towards his siblings. Zelie's face broke into a huge grin.

"I'm so glad I found you guys!" Joseph exclaimed.

"We're so glad to see you!" Zelie said. In her excitement, she started hopping around. "Did you hear the Little Drummer Boy?"

"I did!" Joseph said, suddenly remembering the drum he'd heard when he'd first arrived at the stable. All of the children smiled at the thought that they'd heard the Little Drummer Boy play his drum for Baby Jesus.

"Two days felt like an eternity while we were looking for you," Miriam told Joseph, silently thanking God again for helping the siblings find each other.

"It's only been two days?!" Joseph exclaimed in shock. "I was so sure it'd been a lot longer." It felt like at least a week had passed. Maybe longer.

Joseph felt dazed and confused like he had when he first arrived in the area. He pressed his eyes shut, mentally tallying up how many days had gone by.

The first day I got here, and the angels came. The second day we came to Bethlehem, and I found John Paul and the girls, he counted, running over the list again before he told his sister she was right. After all, she *was* almost always right. He just hated to admit it. He supposed most people with a sometimes-bossy older sister like Miriam felt the same way.

"What should we do now?" Zelie asked, breaking the silence that had followed Joseph's realization.

"Should we show Joseph where we've been staying?" Miriam suggested.

"Yes!" Zelie squealed.

Together the four siblings started to walk over the hill, back towards Bethlehem.

"Oh, Holy Night," John Paul began to sing.

His siblings joined in.

The stars are brightly shining.
It is the night
Of our dear Savior's birth.

The music floated over the hills, through the little town of Bethlehem.

Chapter 11

Over a week had passed, but to Miriam, Joseph, John Paul, and Zelie, it felt like a few days. To other children, their schedule might have become monotonous, but there was always something new that interested them. It could be something like new goods or merchants in the marketplace, or meeting a new friend who came by to visit Felix or Junia and Eve. And they'd made time to explore the town, taking advantage of every unique sight it had to offer.

The marketplace. The large, colorful, sometimes-overwhelming marketplace. That's where the children were getting ready to go early one morning. They were slowly getting used to getting up early, especially Zelie. Zelie had always been an early riser, but now she was getting used to waking up possibly two hours earlier than usual. She seemed to wake up with the market.

Miriam examined a snarled strand of hair. She still didn't know of a good way to brush her hair, so she decided to try finger combing it first. *Ouch,* she thought, trying not to wince. Zelie copied Miriam's motions on her own hair, but when she put on her veil, it looked even worse than before.

"Here. Let me help," Miriam said, stepping in to try finger combing her little sister's hair. She started to gently untangle the snarls towards the bottom, humming softly as she went. After a few minutes, she put Zelie's veil back on and tried to hide the remaining knots. Sighing, she told her sister, "That's as good as it's going to get for now, anyway."

The boys were getting impatient. Miriam noticed that John Paul was starting to fall asleep, sitting with his head resting in his hands. "You ready?" Joseph asked, a hint of irritation in his voice.

"Yep," Zelie said. John Paul yawned.

"Time to get up, sleepyhead," Zelie told him, tapping him lightly on the back. He slowly stood up, yawning as he went. John Paul was the one who could sleep until noon if you let him.

Chickens noisily scratched and pecked around on the road that ran just outside of the old building. Miriam walked out into the early morning light first and looked both ways to make sure no one was coming down the road. There weren't any cars around, but just in case, it was better to be safe than sorry. She motioned for her siblings to cross the road with her.

They scurried across the road and took a turn towards the marketplace. Zelie loved to get up early, but she knew that she probably would never be able to get up as early as Junia and Eve. For there they were already fully awake helping to pick up fruit that had fallen off the stand.

"Here! I'll help!" Zelie called. She ran over to help the girls. With all of the children working together, they made quick work of cleaning up the mess. Junia and Eve's parents smiled to show their appreciation. They were also just naturally good people, who liked to smile often. They reminded Joseph of his teacher, Sister Marie Faustina. She was always smiling, it seemed. She also had a natural talent for making others want to smile. She could always cheer you up. "Let us always meet each other with a smile, for a smile is the beginning of love," she'd say, quoting Mother Teresa. Miriam was sitting closest to Junia and Eve's parents. When there weren't any customers near them, she heard them whispering, and she made out the word "thieves". She knew she shouldn't have been eavesdropping, so she listened more intently to the story Junia was telling about the day Eve was born.

But that one whispered word sent Miriam's brain into panic mode. She had always been the "worry-wart" of the family. Miriam cautiously surveyed the market, searching for anything – or anybody – that looked out of place. All she could see were the friends they had made, and they had gained Miriam's trust. Nothing suspicious. Miriam relaxed, taking a deep breath.

After a few moments, the group heard singing and the sounds of large animals. It sounded like a song about Jesus. In perfect unison, the men sitting atop the camels chanted,

Over the mountains we shall go.
And before the new King kneel!

Junia jumped up and ran to the edge of the road to get a better view of what was happening. Other people had the same idea, and crowds were starting to form along the sides of the road. Camels started walking down the road, carrying people on their backs! It was like a parade.

A sudden realization hit Joseph. *The three wise men!* It was the twelfth day of Christmas, after all. They were coming to see Baby Jesus!

"Guys, look," Joseph said to his siblings. "It's the three wise men! I'm sure of it!"

"Of course!" Miriam said, figuring out his reasoning. "It's been about twelve days since everyone was at the stable."

John Paul wasn't so sure. "They don't look like they do in our nativity scene at home," he said.

"No, but who else could it be?" Zelie replied. "Besides, look how fancy their clothes are!"

It was true – the Wise Men were wearing colorful cloaks that were much fancier than anything the people of Bethlehem wore. Accessories made of gold and various jewels accented their outfits. They also had many people who appeared to be their servants, and their saddle bags were filled to the brim with various riches.

The Wise Men headed down the street, in the direction of the stable.

"What are we waiting for?" Zelie cried. "Let's follow them!" Zelie and John Paul took off through the crowds.

"Guys, wait up!" Miriam called. Joseph followed. Zelie and John Paul ran through the crowds, never losing sight of the camels. She cut through a street and made a couple of turns, so the wise men wouldn't notice her. She and John Paul had almost reached the well in the center of the town when Miriam and Joseph caught up. For once, there wasn't a huge group of people surrounding the well. Out of breath, Zelie and John Paul sat down. They had stitches in their sides.

Miriam and Joseph sat down on the well beside the youngest two Langfords.

"Well, Zelie Louise Langford, you have officially raced the wise men and won," Miriam told her little sister. Joseph nodded.

"Yep," he said. "The crowds are pressing in on them back there."

"I've got to find out if it's really them!" Zelie exclaimed. "If they give Baby Jesus gold, frankincense, and myrrh, I'll know."

"Yeah!" John Paul agreed. "We have to get there so that they don't see us!"

"Okay, but hang on a minute," Miriam said.

"Hang on to what?" Zelie asked with a mischievous grin. Miriam rolled her eyes. Zelie was trying to be difficult on purpose. Little sisters could be *so annoying*.

"Ready to go?" John Paul said a minute later, jumping up from where he was sitting.

"I'm ready as I'll ever be!" Zelie called, already racing towards the stable.

When they got to the stable, they found Mary holding Baby Jesus in her arms, softly singing a lull-aby. It was the most beautiful thing the children had ever heard! Baby Jesus smiled up at her, waving His tiny hands in the air. St. Joseph was bringing in wood from the back of the stable.

Zelie, who had been running as fast as she could, slowed down as she approached the stable. Mary smiled at her, and Zelie enthusiastically smiled back. Mary looked down at Baby Jesus, who smiled at both of them.

Mary sat Baby Jesus up a little higher in her arms. By this time, the other children had caught up. Mary looked at Miriam.

"Would you like to hold Him?" she asked her. Everyone gathered around Miriam as Mary tenderly placed Baby Jesus in her arms. She looked into His small Face with love. After a few moments of Baby Jesus happily sitting in Miriam's arms, Miriam gently handed him back to His Mother.

"I'm Zelie," Zelie announced as everyone sat down around Mary's feet. "This is John Paul, Joseph, and Miriam." Mary nodded, looking at each of the children tenderly as Zelie introduced them. The hem of her gown rustled softly in the breeze. Her blue mantle hung loosely around her shoulders, and Baby Jesus was holding on tightly to her veil.

Not long after, they heard the clip-clop of camels' hooves. Lots of camels' hooves. Possibly *hundreds* of camels' hooves. They were all advancing towards the stable. Three camels stood in front of the rest, holding three men on their backs. Zelie knew, plain as day, that they couldn't be anyone but the wise men. When they arrived at the entrance to the stable, some men who were dressed in plain clothing held the camels' reins while the wise men stepped down. They each took a gilded container out of their saddlebags, then fell to their knees before Baby Jesus.

Joseph's class was making presentations on the wise men, and Miriam's class had done it the previous year. Both Miriam and Joseph immediately recognized the first king to step closer to Baby Jesus as Melchior because he set a box of shining gold near Baby Jesus. He looked much older than the rest – he looked like he was about 60 years old. The next king was Balthasar. He held a censer in front of the manger. Zelie and John Paul, who didn't know that it was called a censer, thought it looked like what Father Peters carried incense in at Mass. Balthasar was younger than Melchior – maybe around 40 years old. The last king to present his gift was Caspar. He was definitely the youngest – he looked like he was around college age. He carried a container that held little rock-like pieces of myrrh.

The sweet, slightly smoky aroma of frankincense and myrrh scented the stable's air. The wise men again fell to their knees. Miriam stood up with her siblings behind her. They waved goodbye to the Holy Family and started to walk down the dusty road back to the town. Mary smiled back at them.

When they were out of earshot, Miriam asked Zelie, "Does that answer your question about the wise men?"

"It was them, definitely," Zelie replied certainly.

The next day, the crowds flooded the roads as they watched the wise men depart. They headed out the direction opposite of the way they came, passing Mordecai on their way back to their home countries.

After holding Baby Jesus, Elisabeth's life changed. She became her joyful self all the time again, not just when guests were looking. She and Thaddeus went back to the stable every day to check on the Holy Family, making sure they had everything they needed.

Baby Jesus always seemed happy to see her, and she was quickly becoming good friends with His mother.

Best of all, sorrow no longer clouded her heart. All of her spare moments were no longer spent grieving over Adam. Instead, she fully committed herself to taking care of the Holy Family, along with the many other guests at the inn. She'd never been happier!

One day, as the mid-winter sun shone down on the earth at full-force, Elisabeth was taking a basket of freshly-baked bread to the Holy Family. When she arrived, Joseph was saddling the donkey as Mary folded laundry, Baby Jesus in her arms. No one needed to tell Elisabeth; she knew the Holy Family was leaving. But she still asked.

Mary nodded, sympathy filling her eyes. Elisabeth stood stock-still, feeling like the sky had fallen on top of her. She knew this day would come – she just hadn't expected it to come this soon. Mary tucked a few other things into a bag.

Mary gently laid her Son in Elisabeth's arms, just like she had done the first day, all the while thanking Elisabeth for everything she'd done for them in her soft, melodic voice. Tears welled up in Elisabeth's eyes as she held Baby Jesus close to her heart for the last time. She swallowed the lump in her throat as she gazed into His tiny face.

Telling Baby Jesus goodbye and handing Him back to His Mother, Elisabeth whispered to Mary, "Please remember that you will always be welcome here in Bethlehem."

Mary nodded, smiling sadly at Elisabeth. Elisabeth hugged them one last time, and then it was time for the Holy Family to leave. Mary sat with Baby Jesus on the donkey, and Joseph started to lead them down the road. Elisabeth, holding her basket, began to walk down the road back to Bethlehem.

In the midst of her sadness, though, Elisabeth felt a calming peace inside of her. She knew that Jesus had touched her heart in a special way. Looking back at the empty stable, Elisabeth let her tears flow down her cheeks, making room for the peace and joy that the Holy Family had left with her.

About a week later, Elisabeth thought fondly of the Holy Family when she realized why Adam's old baby

things still sat in the corner of Thaddeus and Elisabeth's bedroom. Soon, there would be another baby who would need them.

Chapter 12

Miriam, Joseph, John Paul, and Zelie had been visiting the Holy Family every day. They loved spending time with the Holy Family, sitting at Mary's feet and happily playing with Baby Jesus, but they were starting to miss their parents and their dog, Teddy. Teddy was a playful Daisy dog who loved long walks – especially when those long walks ended in a trip to the park near their house. He ate anything he thought looked good, and grass could be considered part of his diet.

That day in Bethlehem, as the weather got progressively warmer, the four were walking along the dusty road to the stable. If Teddy had been there, he would've been trotting up that hill at full speed, wagging his tail enthusiastically. As they approached the stable, Zelie was the first to notice that something was different this time.

"The Holy Family's gone! They took their donkey and left!" Zelie shouted. The others jerked to attention.

"Maybe they just went to get something in the city, or to visit Elisabeth," Joseph suggested. Elisabeth was the innkeeper's wife, and another frequent visitor to the Holy Family. She was one of the sweetest ladies the children had ever met.

"I think Zelie's right, Joseph," Miriam said. "They took all of their things, and I'm sure that they would have left some things if they were only going to be in town for a little while."

"Miriam's right," John Paul agreed.

Just then, the shimmering light appeared, surrounding the children, who were now standing in the middle of the empty stable. Miriam grabbed Zelie's hand and held on tight as the light carried them away. *We're going home*, Miriam thought. She didn't bother saying it out loud, though, because she doubted anyone would hear her.

But Miriam was wrong. When they were standing in daylight again, the siblings were all together this time, but they were *definitely* not in Woodrift. They were on the outskirts of a huge city that looked similar to Bethlehem, just bigger. As a donkey trotted past the children, they caught sight of a woman wearing a familiar pale blue dress. The Holy Family had just ridden by but hadn't noticed them.

"Did you guys just see what I saw?" Miriam asked her siblings. "The Holy Family just rode by!"

"Let's follow them!" Zelie cried.

"Great minds think alike," Miriam said to Zelie. "C'mon, they went that way."

The boys followed Miriam and Zelie. They all made sure to keep a good distance behind the Holy Family, in case they thought that the children had followed them. Technically, they were following them now, but still it would look a little strange.

The Holy Family rounded a corner. Miriam waited for a minute or two, then continued on. The Holy Family went through a stone gate. When the four children caught up and passed through the gate, they saw the Holy Family just ahead of them, with Mary dismounting from the donkey. Two women stood beside them. Miriam heard one of the women call the older one Anna. Anna was tall and had gray hair that was streaked with white. She didn't know who the other was, until Anna called her Noemi.

St. Joseph lifted down the baskets filled with fruit and the two turtledoves. He handed them to Anna, and then tied up the donkey in a small shed on the other side of the courtyard. Mary, Baby Jesus, Anna, and Noemi went inside the temple. Joseph followed them, and the children followed him.

They didn't know where everyone else had gone, but the four didn't feel like following St. Joseph again. Instead, they walked in the other direction, towards the back of the stone temple. The temple wasn't very big; in fact, the courtyard was much larger than the building itself. In the back of the temple were small cells with stone floors. They were furnished sparsely due to their miniature size.

Inside one of the rooms, an old man knelt on the floor. He had a long, pale gray beard.

"I wonder if that's Simeon," Miriam whispered to her siblings. Simeon was too concentrated on praying to notice them, and they walked on down the hallway.

"Let's turn back the other way," Zelie said. "It must be about time for the Presentation in the Temple to happen."

"Yeah, I definitely don't want to miss that," Joseph replied.

The children quietly started walking back in the direction they came. John Paul looked in Simeon's cell; he wasn't there. John Paul wondered where he'd disappeared to so quickly.

At the end of the hallway, they turned and walked into a large hall. St. Joseph was sitting in the back with some other men, while Mary and Baby Jesus were sitting in the front of the area with about 20 other women. Miriam froze. None of the Langford children had been in a temple before, and with a special ceremony going on....where would they sit? Miriam decided to just stand in the back. It seemed like the safest option.

On the altar were several lamps and a table. The priests' vestments were neatly laid on top of the table. Priests sat around the room in prayer. Bowls of blood sat around the temple. When Zelie noticed them, she made a gagging noise in the back of her throat. Miriam grabbed her arm, silently telling her to stop and trying to resist the urge to elbow her little sister in the ribs.

Simeon stood near the Holy Family. Mary handed Baby Jesus to Simeon to hold. Simeon held Him close and said, "Now, Master, you may let your servant go in peace, according to your word, for my eyes have seen your salvation, which you prepared in sight of all the peoples, a light for revelation to the Gentiles, and glory for your people Israel."

He then turned to Mary and said, "Behold, this child is destined for the fall and rise of many in Israel, and to be a sign that will be contradicted, and you yourself a sword will pierce, so that the thoughts of many hearts may be revealed." Anna stepped forward and joyfully blessed God, thanking Him for letting her see the Messiah.

Simeon stepped forward, with Mary and Baby Jesus behind him. A priest held Baby Jesus up for everyone to see. Simeon took a scroll and prayed over Mary and Baby Jesus. Afterwards, he led Mary and Jesus back to the area where the women sat, and Anna sat beside them.

The priests burned incense and prayed aloud. The sweet, smoky incense floated throughout the temple. As Mary cradled Baby Jesus in her arms, her face shone.

At the end of the day, the exhausted kids were traveling back to Nazareth. With a few coins Miriam had miraculously found in her bag, which was attached to the waist of her dress, she bought some food before leaving Jerusalem.

"Don't eat too much," Miriam warned her siblings as the hungry travelers rested for the night under a large tree. "We have to make this food last until we get back to a city."

The children laid out their mantles, and the girls laid out their veils. They slept underneath the leafy overhang, and as soon as the sun came up, they were well-rested and ready to walk wherever they needed to go. The Holy Family had been sleeping a little ways ahead of them. They put on their mantles and veils, and they started to walk down the road.

When they passed the place where the Holy Family had slept the night before, they saw that Jesus, Mary, and Joseph had already left.

"Great," Joseph muttered under his breath. "Now what do we do?"

"We'll pray and keep going," Miriam said confidently. "We'll find a way out, just like you and Silas found your way out of the forest."

And so they were off. They walked beside grassy hills and through resting fields. Zelie and John Paul splashed through the shallow stream, kicking up water and getting everything wet.

"Zelie, I think you should take off your veil," Miriam suggested. "It's too chilly out to wear something wet."

Shivering, Zelie peeled off her veil and handed it to Miriam. She and John Paul also took off their mantles. Joseph stopped them, pointing to a spot a little farther upstream. A donkey was drinking from the stream while a couple held a baby and sat under a tree.

"Well, we've found them," John Paul said.

"This is perfect!" Miriam exclaimed. "We can take a little break, make a plan, and most importantly, let your clothes dry." Zelie grabbed the garments and laid them in a dry spot on the hill. Then she sat next to her siblings. Joseph and John Paul were scrubbing the dirt off their hands by the stream.

When the Holy Family continued on their journey, so did the four siblings.

The next afternoon, everyone arrived in Nazareth. The children had lots of fun "camping," even if they were lacking the things they used to go camping in the summer. If they had ridden to Nazareth, they would have had more energy, but Miriam, for one, was ready to settle down and take a break.

"Where should we stay?" She asked her siblings, who were eager to find a place to rest for the night.

"Let's just hang out in an old building like we did the last time," Zelie said.

"Well, pray to St. Joseph that we'll find it," Miriam replied, somewhat doubting that there were that many abandoned buildings around. A teacher had mentioned once that St. Joseph was the patron saint of realtors, and one time, when they moved to a new house when Miriam was seven, Joseph was four and John Paul was 6 months old, their parents had prayed to St. Joseph to find them a house.

Sure enough, they found a tiny old shack that was ironically about a block away from the Holy Family's house! "Your prayers worked, Zelie," John Paul said. All of the kids were amazed by this miracle.

"Thank-you, St. Joseph," Miriam whispered. Why had she ever doubted?

And so, it came to be that the Langfords found their way to Nazareth.

Chapter 13

Zelie yawned loudly. John Paul rolled over and fell asleep. Miriam and Joseph, well-rested, started to sit up.

"Let's go explore," Zelie said, already bouncing around.

"Let's let John Paul sleep," Miriam replied.

"No, I'm up," John Paul said sleepily, stretching his legs.

The girls adjusted their veils, and they left to explore Nazareth.

"I like it here better than in Bethlehem," Zelie said, reaching up to run her hand along a rough mud brick. "It's calmer."

"Probably less people, since the census is pretty much over," John Paul told her.

"Hey, look, another well," Zelie observed. Sure enough, there was a well with a thick crowd of women talking around it. They noticed that Mary was among the crowd, filling up her jug as she talked with a few other women standing around her. The children decided not to linger and continued on with their walk, trying not to make many turns so that they wouldn't get lost.

For the people who lived there, it seemed to be a pretty normal day in Nazareth. There were women cooking, children playing, and men working. Soon they decided to turn back, going down a different street. There they saw someone they recognized.

St. Joseph was carving something out of wood. He seemed to be about done when the children came to the building. He started to hammer it onto another wooden piece.

Zelie stood on tiptoes, trying to get a better view. "Can you see what he's making?" she asked her siblings. They were a lot taller than she was; maybe they would be able to see better.

"I'm not sure yet," Miriam told her sister.

"Maybe a stool?" Joseph said.

Just then, a customer walked into the shop.

"I'm just about done," they heard St. Joseph tell the man. "I'm putting on the final touches."

Mary came in just then, holding Baby Jesus and carrying her jug.

"That's beautiful, Joseph!" she exclaimed in her melodic, gentle way. She smiled at him. Jesus clapped his tiny hands.

"Just what I was going to say," the man agreed.

St. Joseph held up the finished stool and handed it to the customer. He paid St. Joseph and walked away, thanking him heartily.

As the man walked away, the children got a better glimpse of the stool. It was intricately carved and was as close to perfect as a stool could ever get.

"That's amazing!" John Paul breathed.

"Yeah," Zelie said. "Too bad we don't have the money to buy some."

"Come on, guys," Miriam told her siblings, reminding them that they were standing in the middle of the road. "Let's keep walking."

The next day, the children, adventurous as ever, set out to explore a different part of town. People were talking everywhere in low, hushed voices about thieves in the area.

"I heard that they killed someone a few towns over," one woman whispered to another, her voice fearful.

"I just hope they won't hurt anyone here," the other woman whispered back.

"There's thieves around here?!" Zelie whispered to her siblings, her eyes growing wide in fear. Miriam nodded, confessing that she'd heard Junia and Eve's parents talking about the thieves when they were still in Bethlehem.

"Don't worry, Zelie," John Paul said, trying to comfort his little sister. "If the thieves try to touch a hair on your head, I'll kick their butts."

Zelie smiled at that. Both John Paul and Joseph were wrestlers – and they were good at it, too. Their room was full of trophies, medals, and plaques that told of their numerous achievements at wrestling meets.

From that day on, every time they heard a noise, if it was the wind blowing against their shed or some kind of animal noise, the four kids immediately woke up worrying about the thieves. Occasionally, one of them would open the door just a crack and peek out. Whenever sleep finally came, it wouldn't last long.

This pattern went on for a couple of nights until another noise woke them up in the night.

The sound of babies and toddlers' wails echoed through the town. Soldiers walked down different streets, going uninvited into people's homes. If they found any babies or toddlers under two, they took them away.

That night, Miriam, Joseph, John Paul, and Zelie tried to ignore the noise and sleep. About an hour after her siblings had fallen asleep, Miriam was still awake. The despairing sounds that had seemed to envelop the town earlier were becoming fainter and fainter. Miriam relaxed, relieved that the terrible soldiers seemed to be leaving.

An animal's *clip-clop, clip-clop* of hooves sounded on the pavement, waking up Joseph. Miriam saw a piece of blue fabric through a crack in the door and knew at once who it belonged to.

"Did you see what I just saw?" Miriam asked Joseph.

"Yeah. Let's follow them," Joseph replied. Miriam and Joseph woke up their younger siblings. "The Holy Family is leaving!" they said, shaking Zelie and John Paul awake.

For once, John Paul was fully awake. Zelie sprung into action. "Let's follow them!" She exclaimed excitedly.

"Exactly what we had in mind," Joseph told her, looking at Miriam.

"Let's go – we're wasting time," Miriam said. Without another word, they slipped out of the shed. They didn't realize it then, but they wouldn't return to the shed again.

They climbed up the hill, following the Holy Family a safe distance away. Suddenly, Miriam and Joseph pulled Zelie and John Paul back, covering their mouths.

"Thieves," Joseph whispered. John Paul nodded. He held his finger to his mouth.

A thief, a young man with thick, dark hair, approached St. Joseph. "Let me see your Child and I'll let you pass," the children heard him say. St. Joseph held his staff in between him and the thief. Mary nodded, so St. Joseph let him pass.

When he looked down at Baby Jesus, his rough expression changed. He knelt down before Him and said, "Lord, if ever in this life I need your friendship, please come to my aid."

Zelie smiled, remembering the legend from a book at their house. The thief would later be known as "the good thief" who was crucified beside Jesus and asked for His mercy then. The thief left, empty-handed. When he disappeared behind the hills, Jesus, Mary, and Joseph continued on their journey. Baby Jesus cuddled closer to Mary as St. Joseph stopped the donkey inside of a cave.

Miriam pointed to an area behind the cave, and the children sat down there to rest. Suddenly, they heard the sound of a soldier. Miriam's heart raced. She hoped the soldiers wouldn't hear its pounding and come to investigate. But, miraculously, they didn't even seem to notice the cave was there!

John Paul stood up and started to walk to the front of the cave. His siblings followed. There it was – still open to everyone from the outside, just like it had been when the Holy Family went inside. Mary and St. Joseph were both asleep, but as the four children gazed inside, they noticed that Baby Jesus was awake. His tiny face stretched into a tiny smile. He seemed happy to see them.

That's when the light returned and whisked them away.

Chapter 14

There they were. Fully intact, thank goodness, and back in their school uniforms, inside the small chapel full of reliquaries.

"Did that really just happen, or did I imagine it all?" John Paul asked.

"No, it really happened," Zelie replied. "I still have my veil." It was true. She held in her hands the same linen veil that had covered her head in Bethlehem, and then in Nazareth.

"It's the exact same time we left – 3:45," Miriam said, looking down at her watch. "Mom will be here to pick us up soon."

"Wow," Joseph said, amazed and shocked and in disbelief, all at the same time.

"You can say that again," Miriam agreed.

"If we go out that door, will the church still be outside?" Joseph wondered.

"Oh my gosh, I hope so," Zelie said, her voice shaking a little with the last syllable. "I hadn't even thought about that."

"I wonder if I'll ever see Junia and Eve again," she continued after a minute's pause.

Miriam smiled. "Probably not, Zelie. I think that we just time traveled back from two thousand years ago."

"Two thousand years?!" Joseph exclaimed. "I kind of forgot it was that long ago."

"Me, too," John Paul agreed.

Miriam put her hand on the doorknob. She was again a little afraid to open it. She took a deep breath and turned the knob. Relieved, she stepped out into the Immaculate Heart of Mary parish church.

Their backpacks were still where they had left them in the first pew. Zelie tucked her veil carefully into the front pocket of her book bag.

As they turned to leave, Zelie pointed at the door to the chapel. It was enveloped in light. A shimmer went down it from top to bottom, and when the light touched the ground, the door disappeared completely. The children looked at each other in amazement.

Together, the four children genuflected in front of the altar, and made their way out of the church. It was still lightly snowing. Zelie and John Paul stuck out their tongues to catch snowflakes.

Just then, their mom's blue SUV pulled up in the driveway.

"Hi, guys," she greeted them. "How was your day at school?"

"It was good," Miriam said. The other children echoed her response.

"Sorry it took a little longer today," she told them, stopping at the traffic light. "Lisa and Julie needed some extra help setting up the new exhibit that's coming in from Chicago, since we were a little short-staffed today. Did you get awfully cold waiting out there?"

"Well, we went into the church for a little while," John Paul said. "But we were fine outside. After all, a little fresh air never hurt anyone."

His siblings laughed, and their mother smiled, not quite understanding the joke. Before they knew it, they were pulling into their own driveway.

Miriam and Zelie brought their backpacks into the bedroom they shared. Miriam needed to do homework, but Zelie needed to make sure she found a safe place for her veil.

"Why don't you put it on the shelf in the closet?" Miriam suggested, pulling out a pencil.

"Nah, it might fall off," Zelie replied.

"What about the top dresser drawer?" Miriam asked.

"Good idea!" Zelie agreed. She gingerly placed the veil in the top drawer that was reserved for the Langford sisters' most special possessions.

"Hey Miriam?"

"Yeah?"

"I don't think we should tell anyone about what just happened—yet."

"Okay," Miriam said. She'd been thinking the same thing. After all, how could they tell someone that they'd time traveled to the First Christmas? She imagined what her parents' reaction would be like. That would certainly be a strange thing to hear from your children!

"I'll go tell the boys," Zelie told her sister, bringing Miriam out of her daydream.

She found the boys in the living room, watching TV with Teddy sitting on the couch beside them. She hopped up on the couch next to John Paul and delivered the message. Then she skipped back to her bedroom, hopping onto the beanbag to read until suppertime.

After Christmas Mass, the four Langfords gathered around the Nativity scene at the front of the church for their annual picture.

"One, two, three, smile!" Their mom prompted, holding up her cell phone. They all put on their nicest smiles and looked toward the camera.

"Alright. Good job, guys," their mom told them, putting her phone back in her purse. She and their dad started to walk out of the church, but the four children lingered a moment longer, gazing down at

Baby Jesus's smiling face and outstretched arms, and remembering when they knelt before the manger in Bethlehem.

Points of Reference

Biblical:

Chapter 6

> "Do not be afraid; for behold, I proclaim to you good news of great joy that will be for all the people. For today in the city of David a savior has been born for you who is Messiah and Lord. And this will be a sign for you: you will find an infant wrapped in swaddling clothes and lying in a manger." (Luke 2:10-12, NAB)

> "Glory to God in the highest and on earth peace to those on whom his favor rests." (Luke 2:14, NAB)

Chapter 12

> Now, Master, you may let your servant go in peace, according to your word, for my eyes have seen your salvation, which you prepared in sight of all the peoples, a light for revelation to the Gentiles, and glory for your people Israel." (Luke 2:29-32, NAB)

> "Behold, this child is destined for the fall and rise of many in Israel, and to be a sign that will be contradicted and you yourself a sword will pierce so that the

thoughts of many hearts may be revealed." (Luke 2:34-35, NAB)

The Revelations of Blessed Anne Catherine Emmerich:

Chapter 11

"Over the mountains we shall go. And before the new King kneel!" https://tandfspi.org/ACE_vol_01/ACE_1_0241_out.html, p. 250.

Music:

Chapter 10:

- "Soon And Very Soon" by Andrae Edward Crouch
- "O Holy Night" by Placide Cappeau and Adolphe Adam

Inspirations:

- Fontanini
- *The Thief Who Stole Heaven* by Raymond Arroyo.
- The Little Drummer Boy

Acknowledgments

When I think back on *The Children of the Chapel and the First Christmas* and my writing journey, I remember that there are so many incredible people who have helped Miriam, Joseph, John Paul and Zelie's story become a reality. You have all been such a blessing to have in my life- not only for your help with my book, but for your support, as well. I truly treasure all of you, and I couldn't have done it without you!

First, I'd like to thank my parents. You have done so much for me, and you are the reason why I'm writing these acknowledgments today! Thank-you for teaching me about God and instilling in me a love for my Faith from the very beginning, and thank-you for encouraging me in everything I've ever attempted to do and celebrating with me in everything I've ever accomplished. I owe a special debt of gratitude to my mom, who has edited with me countless times and has given me lots of advice and guidance for this book. I love you both so much!

I also need to thank my brothers, Noah and Caleb. You have always listened to my crazy ideas and dreams, and you were some of the first people to hear The Children of the Chapel and the First Christmas come to life. I love you!

Grandma and Grandpa and Grandma Eleanor, you have been listening to my stories and applauding them since I first started writing as a little girl, and for that, I will always be grateful. On top of that, you also helped me write more stories and poems, providing me with a typewriter to practice on and lots of art supplies to make illustrations to accompany my writing. Grandma and Grandma Eleanor also helped me edit this book and provided helpful suggestions. Thank-you for supporting me and for being the best grandparents a girl could ever ask for!

This book would not have come together without the help from so many wonderful people who generously gave of their time! I would love to mention you all by name, but I am afraid I would miss someone. Thank-you to those who helped to edit the book, gave suggestions to help me get past a period of writers' block, encouraged me in my writing, and those who have prayed for me during this journey. All of these things have meant so much to me!

I'd also like to thank Sebastian Mahfood at En Route Books and Media. When I first met Sebastian,

I knew I'd finally found the "pearl of great price" of publishers. I know now, without a doubt, that God had a plan and was leading me to En Route!

And to my amazing illustrator, Lora Schaunaman, thank-you for using your talents to glorify God and bring these characters to life!

Finally, and most importantly, I'd like to thank God for the gift of this story. Although it wasn't always easy, I know He was there with me every step of the way. It is my prayer that *The Children of the Chapel and the First Christmas will* bring glory to Him!

About the Author

As a baby, nothing made E. G. Enga happier than having her parents read to her. Before she turned two years old, she taught herself to read and has loved anything and everything to do with literature ever since. She fell in love with writing stories and poetry in Kindergarten and first grade. At the age of 12, she wrote her first published book, *The Children of the Chapel and the First Christmas*, combining her love for her Faith and literature in her writing. She lives in the Midwest with her parents, brothers, and Daisy Dog, Paddington (the real-life Teddy). When she grows up, she wants to fill her house with books, quilts, and lace curtains, and hopes to continue writing books for children.